Raggedy Ann's
Book of Thanks

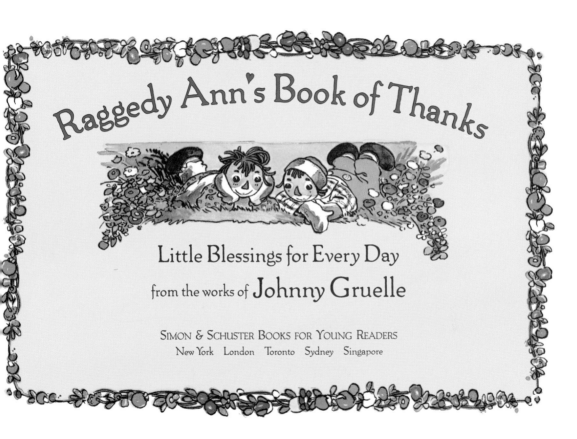

Raggedy Ann's Book of Thanks

Little Blessings for Every Day

from the works of **Johnny Gruelle**

SIMON & SCHUSTER BOOKS FOR YOUNG READERS

New York   London   Toronto   Sydney   Singapore

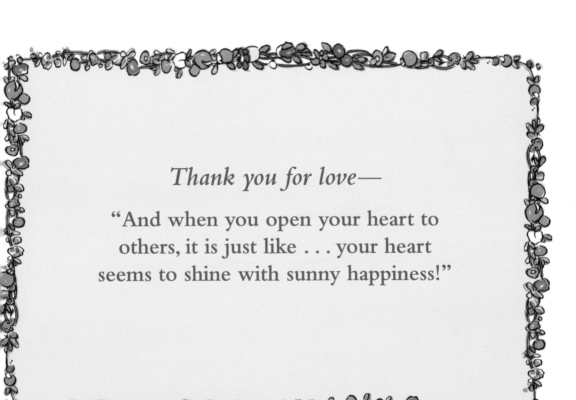

Thank you for love—

"And when you open your heart to others, it is just like . . . your heart seems to shine with sunny happiness!"

Thank you for trust—

"... anyone who loves you can be trusted!"

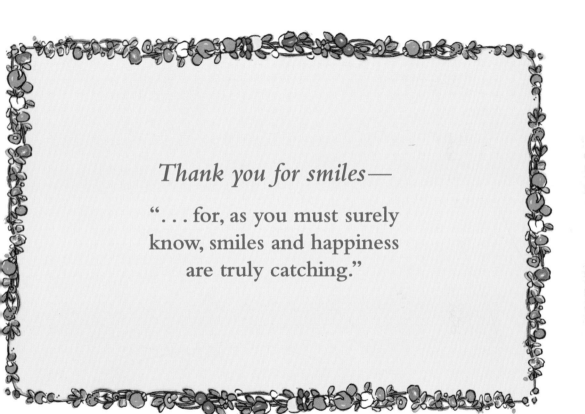

Thank you for smiles—

"...for, as you must surely
know, smiles and happiness
are truly catching."

Thank you for freckles—

"Every little freckle is a sign that a Brownie has kissed a child he loves!"

Thank you for giving—

"For, as you must surely know, they
who are the most unselfish are the ones
who gain the greatest joy; because they
give happiness to others."

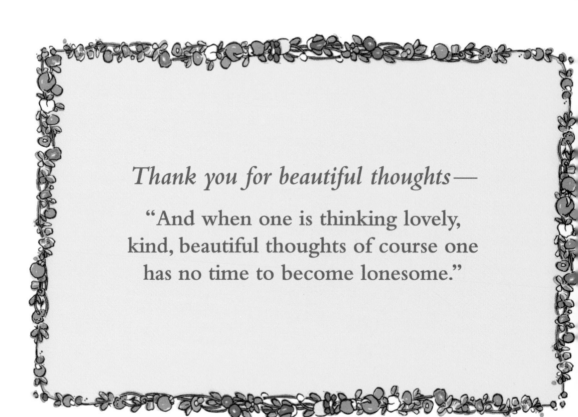

Thank you for beautiful thoughts—

"And when one is thinking lovely, kind, beautiful thoughts of course one has no time to become lonesome."

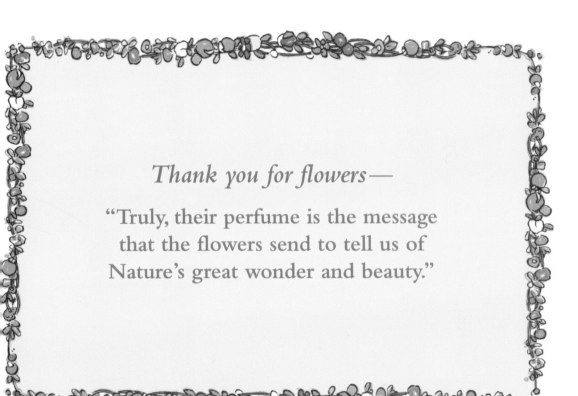

Thank you for flowers—

"Truly, their perfume is the message
that the flowers send to tell us of
Nature's great wonder and beauty."

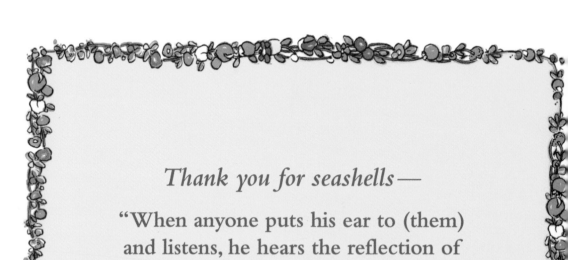

Thank you for seashells—

"When anyone puts his ear to (them) and listens, he hears the reflection of his own heart's music, singing. . . ."

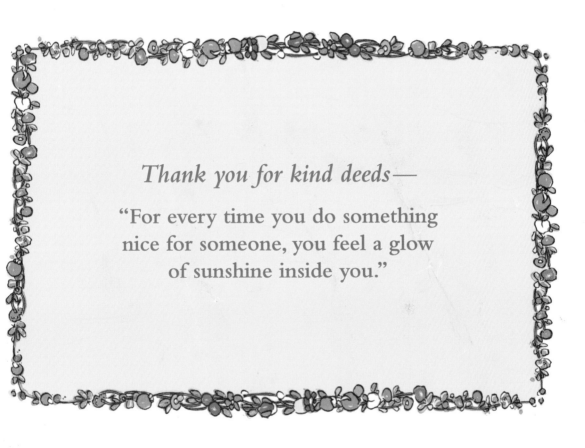

Thank you for kind deeds—

"For every time you do something nice for someone, you feel a glow of sunshine inside you."

Thank you for good friends—

"... for there is nothing that brings such happiness as loving friendship."

Thank you for playtime—

"The more fun we can give each other,
the more fun each one of us will have!"

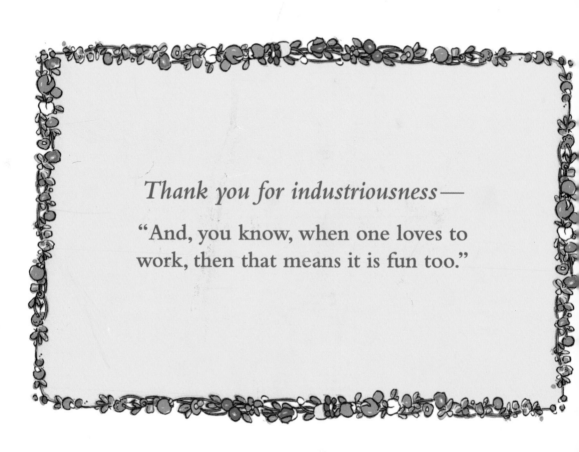

Thank you for industriousness—

"And, you know, when one loves to work, then that means it is fun too."

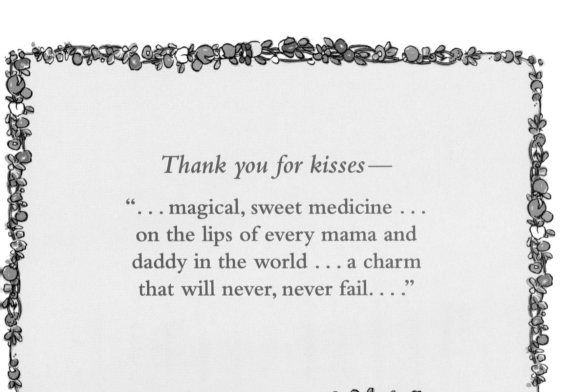

Thank you for kisses —

"... magical, sweet medicine ...
on the lips of every mama and
daddy in the world ... a charm
that will never, never fail. ..."

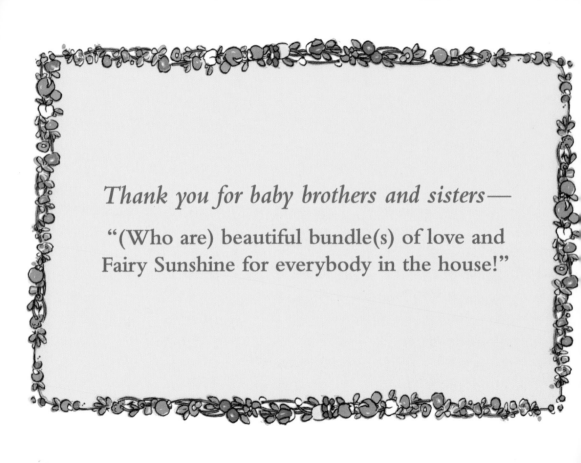

Thank you for baby brothers and sisters—

"(Who are) beautiful bundle(s) of love and Fairy Sunshine for everybody in the house!"

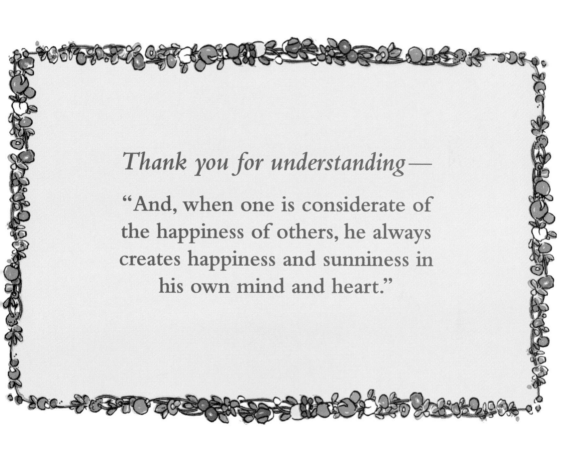

Thank you for understanding—

"And, when one is considerate of the happiness of others, he always creates happiness and sunniness in his own mind and heart."

Thank you for surprises—

"...it is fun to make other people
happy even if they do not know
we are doing it!"

Thank you for happiness—

"It's like a whole lot of sunshine
coming into a dark room. . . ."

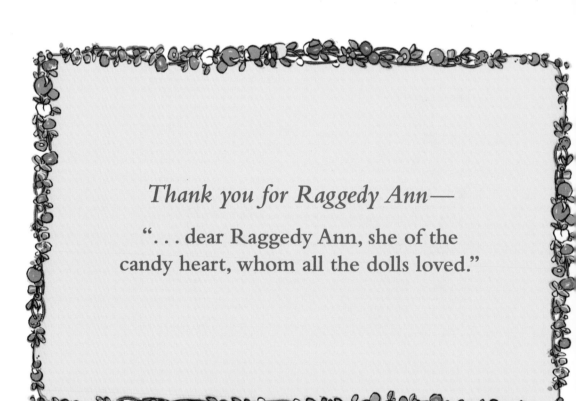

Thank you for Raggedy Ann—

". . . dear Raggedy Ann, she of the
candy heart, whom all the dolls loved."

SIMON & SCHUSTER BOOKS FOR YOUNG READERS
An imprint of Simon & Schuster Children's Publishing Division
1230 Avenue of the Americas, New York, New York 10020

Many of the images in this collection were created in the style of Johnny Gruelle by his brother, Justin Gruelle, and his son, Worth Gruelle. Their devotion to carry on the tradition of Raggedy Ann can be seen in *Raggedy Ann and the Golden Butterfly, Raggedy Ann and the Happy Meadow,* and *Raggedy Ann and the Golden Ring.*